THE CLAIBORNE CURSE

CASTIEL SKULL

For my cousin, Ashley Hamilton. Thank you for helping me
bring the town of Kosher Harbor to life, even if the damn place
is cursed.

CHAPTER 1

JUNE 2006

The town of Kosher Harbor was a gem, hidden in the sands of time. Tourists were few and slim. Not many people in the world even knew Kosher Harbor existed. The residents who lived here enjoyed the peaceful atmosphere and the open skies.

"I hate this damn town," Cecelia spat, talking to no one but herself.

Sometimes, Kosher Harbor wasn't as kosher as it seemed. The town itself was shaped like a jagged letter "M" and at the far-left bottom corner of the town was the lower-class district. The homes in this area were mostly mobile homes. The trailers were stacked on cinder blocks with cheap skirting at the bottom to give the illusion that these flimsy rectangular homes were on a foundation.

Cecelia Claiborne was sitting on her couch, smoking her last menthol cigarette. She listened as children rode their bicycles up and down her street, laughing and yelling out to one another as they played. She hated the month of June. Schools were finally out, and the kids would run wild all day and night long. She even almost hit one with her van fifteen minutes ago when one of the kids tried racing across the street as she turned into the trailer park. She'd just got back from seeing the doctor about her recurring knee pain. She needed a knee replacement, but to her dismay, her doctor refused to schedule one until she lost at least forty pounds. He had said her heart might not be able to handle surgery at her current weight. To hell with that, Cecelia thought to herself.

She continued sulking about her throbbing knee when there was a knock on the flimsy front door. She let out a sigh in annoyance. It was only 3:15PM on a Tuesday. The person knocking was someone unexpected. Someone who would bring her nothing but stress, possibly anger, and make her miserable life suck that much more. She was sure of it.

Cecelia wasn't in the mood to hear any complaints about the condition of her yard, hear any kids ask her to buy cookies, or listen to her neighbors try to invite her to participate in the annual neighborhood yard sale. She'd told them no twice already.

The uninvited guest knocked again. Cecelia rose to her feet, her bones popping with each step, and walked to the door. She looked out the peephole and saw a familiar figure, one she hadn't seen in years. It was her husband.

School, friends, family, and dreams were all forgotten when Brenden Claiborne entered Cecelia's life, forty years ago. She was only fifteen at the time, but she fell for him hard nonetheless. He came into her life like a hurricane, drowning her in toxic waters that she was never able to escape. And she never wanted to for that matter.

They were both enamored with each other from the first day they met. Brenden was four years older than Cecelia, and she believed his experiences in life were far greater than her own. After just a month of dating, they ran off and eloped.

Over the years, neither of them ever worked. Instead, they lived a free life. Free from routine and structure. Free from responsibilities. And they enjoyed it.

They ate peyote in the desert, having the most beautiful hallucinations together. They dropped acid under the stars, willing their minds to expand and share a singular consciousness. They shot heroin in the mountains, and felt snakes biting their veins. They drank absinthe, and chased it with cheap vodka. The trips their minds took didn't require a steady routine, or even a steady environment. If anything, those things would have restricted the travels within their own minds.

They traveled to Kosher Harbor after hearing stories and rumors from a friend, and decided to check it out. Once they arrived, they met a man at a shady bar on the coastline, and he hooked them up with a dealer that specialized in psychedelic drugs, which was their drug subclass of choice. He offered them ayahuasca and mescaline, with a pinch of "something extra" in exchange for the cocaine they had.

They got high in the cemetery that night, hoping to expand their minds enough to see ghosts, but instead saw only the ghosts of who they had once been. They were both in their forties, sitting on the damp ground, leaning against a hard marble tombstone, and shivering. Whatever the "something extra" was, it messed with their minds, making it seem as if they were of one mind, spiritually connected. It scared the hell out of them both and ruined their high. It was that night they decided the lifestyle they were living no longer held the same appeal as it did before.

Tired of seeing ghosts, they decided it was time to settle down. The drifter lifestyle was getting harder on both of them, both physically and mentally. Neither one of them had the money to travel anywhere else, so they'd just stayed in Kosher Harbor. Brenden found a job at a factory in town, and Cecelia found part time work at the hotel they were staying at. It took a few weeks, but they were able to save enough for a single wide trailer in Green Pines, a mobile home community in the lower-class district of Kosher Harbor.

As the years passed, Cecelia made their trailer into a home and fell into a comfortable routine. She actually enjoyed being a stay-at-home trophy wife. However, Brenden became restless. And then, three years ago, he left, leaving Cecelia with no one.

The rumors were what had originally drawn Cecelia and Brenden to Kosher Harbor. When Brenden disappeared, Cecelia found herself in a web of rumors throughout the trailer park. Most of her neighbors said that he had run off with another woman. Others said he'd been drunk and drowned during a midnight swim. There were always stories and speculation about what happened to Brenden. Cecelia knew he'd been restless though, and she knew his leaving was by his own choice. She told him several times before if he left, he better not ever come back to face her wrath.

And now, here he stood.

Cecelia opened the door, her eyes already narrowed. "What the fuck are you doing here?"

"I've come home to die," Brenden said, smiling weakly. He opened his arms, inviting her into them.

Cecelia stood motionless for a few moments, varying emotions surging through her veins. They were bubbling up and it overwhelmed her. She burst into tears and fell into his arms. Brenden held her and soothed her as she cried. "You dirty dog," she sobbed, clinging to him. She was torn between wanting to hate him and wanting to love him. And right now, all she could do was let her emotions escape in the form of tears, and cling to the one who had been her security for so many years.

"Can I come in?" he asked, stroking her long black hair that was in its normal braid.

Cecelia sniffed, and considered his request. She'd barely survived the years he was gone, but she did survive. It was hard to do it alone, but it might be just as hard with him back in her life, perhaps harder. The thought of slamming the door in his face crossed her mind. However, the loss she knew she would feel shutting him out made her impulsively step back into the trailer, making room for Brenden to follow behind her.

"The place looks the same," Brenden remarked, looking around.

It did look the same. Cecelia had lost the additional income Brenden provided when he left, and her disability wasn't enough for any major redecorating. Their wedding photo, both were wearing jeans and barefoot, was still hanging on the wall above the kitchen table.

Cecelia stared at him, not knowing what to say. A thousand questions came to mind, but her throat could form no words. For a moment, the old man that stood before her became the young man she'd fallen so madly in love with. She shook her head to clear the image, and only then noticed how much Brenden had aged during his absence.

His dark hair was graying, and his skin had a pale, waxy appearance to it. His eyes were sunken and dark, and his breathing was labored. He said he'd come home to die. Was he sick? An uneasy feeling pushed its way into the back of Cecelia's mind. *Why'd I let him in?*

CHAPTER 2

Cecelia drove across Kosher Harbor to the business district. At the seafood market, she visited Sophie's Seafood Sensations to buy some fresh fish. She wanted to prepare Brenden a homecoming meal. She bought a whole grouper and two pounds of clams. The weather was dreary and damp, just like her mood. As she waited for her seafood to be wrapped and rang up, Cecelia's mind drifted to the man waiting for her at home.

She asked him where he'd been, and he claimed he didn't remember. All he said was he was near water and the place was dirty. Cecelia had quickly become annoyed with his vague responses, and changed the subject, asking him what he meant when he said he'd come home to die. Brenden was vague with answering that line of questioning as well, stating that he just didn't feel well and didn't think he had much time left. All he knew was he needed to make his way home to be with the woman he loved for his final days. He couldn't explain anything past an instinctual level.

Cecelia thanked Sophie when she received her bundle of fish, ignoring the old woman trying to give her instructions for dressing the grouper. She'd lived in Kosher Harbor for almost fifteen years now. Seafood was a major food source in the town, and she knew how to prepare fish. She'd seen Sophie on a weekly basis for those fifteen years, and the old woman never remembered who she was. Cecelia wondered if Sophie had memory issues. She must have. Who else handles fish while wearing a diamond ring? She must have forgotten to take it off.

Arriving back home, Cecelia found Brenden sitting on the old brown couch that was in their living room. He was staring at the television, but it was turned off. He didn't look up or seem to notice her enter the trailer.

"I'm back," Cecelia said, scowling at him. If she was going to welcome him back into her life after three damn years, he could at least give her the courtesy of acknowledging her when she came in.

Brenden turned his head slowly and looked up to Cecelia; his movements were sluggish.

"Are you drunk?" she demanded. If he thought he'd just waltz back into her life to lay around and drink, he had another thing coming.

"No," Brenden answered, his eyes rolling around in his head as he answered.

Cecelia's eyes narrowed into small slits at his perceived deception, ready to tear into him, but then she eased off. Brenden didn't look drunk, he looked sick. "I'll call Dr. Hanus tomorrow. You look like hell." Dr. Hanus had a private practice in Kosher Harbor. There were no other doctors in the town. You had to go out of Kosher Harbor for extensive testing or surgery.

"I feel like hell. I feel like I swallowed a mouthful of dirt," Brenden said, his voice thick.

"I'll get you a drink. Do you want chocolate milk?" Cecelia asked. Since she'd given up alcohol five years ago, she developed an addiction to chocolate milk. She talked Brenden into giving up drinking as well, but who knows if he stayed on the wagon during the three years he was missing.

"Yeah," Brenden replied, his throat cracking.

Cecelia moved into the kitchen, sitting the bag of fish and clams on the counter. She pulled the refrigerator door open and took out a gallon of chocolate milk. After pouring a huge amount into a plastic double gulp cup she saved from the gas station, she handed it to Brenden. He began to drink, and didn't pause to breathe until the entire sixty-four-ounce cup was empty.

Cecelia watched in disgust. When Brenden finished the milk, he held the empty cup out to Cecelia and requested water. She filled the enormous cup with water from the kitchen tap, and gave it back to him. He drank half of it before resting the cup on his thigh.

"I needed that," Brenden said. He wiped his mouth with the back of his hand.

"You're welcome," Cecelia sarcastically remarked, irritated that he didn't thank her.

She took a roll of aluminum foil out of a drawer and spread it on the table that sat in the corner of the kitchen. Unwrapping the grouper, she placed it on the foil, and then got the supplies she needed to prepare the fish.

"Where have you been?" Cecelia asked, once again trying to get information out of Brenden. She wanted to know as his wife, but it would also be important to have those details to share with the doctor. Using a dull knife, she started scraping the scales off the grouper.

"I told you. I can't remember. Everything is hazy. All I know is it wasn't a good place, and I'm glad to be back home," Brenden answered. He brought the double gulp cup back to his mouth and finished off the water.

"That's not a good enough answer. Because the whole damn town thinks you ran off with some whore, and truthfully Brenden, I think the same. I don't want to look like a damn fool taking you back into my life."

"Since when do you care about gossip?" Brenden asked.

"Since my good-for-nothing husband disappeared on me and I became the center of it," Cecelia snapped. She finished scaling the fish, and picked up a meat cleaver.

"I wasn't with any woman," Brenden defended, although his voice wasn't strong.

"You sure as hell weren't with me," Cecelia said, pointing the cleaver at Brenden.

"I'm always with you, Babe. We're spiritually connected."

"Hallucinogens didn't meld our minds together, Brenden." Cecelia swung the cleaver down, chopping the grouper's head off. She turned the headless fish, and used the cleaver to sever the pectoral fins with clean chops.

Brenden jumped each time the cleaver landed, seeing the parts of the fish become separated from its body.

"I've always felt your presence," Brenden said, finding his voice once Cecelia stopped chopping.

"That was just the drugs. I didn't feel any damn presence while you were gone. I felt nothing but heartache and misery. I missed you, you son-of-a-bitch," Cecelia spat. She wasn't sure who she was angrier with, herself or Brenden. She had every right to be angry with Brenden for leaving her, and she had every right to be angry with herself for still loving him.

She took her anger out on the grouper, splitting its belly with the dull knife. Its entrails spilled out onto the table, just below their wedding portrait that hung on the wall above the table.

"I missed you too. I don't think I should have, but I did," Brenden said. His head fell against the back of the couch. "Do you have to do that right there? I'm feeling a little queasy."

"And where would you like me to do it? Be a man," Cecelia spat, pulling the viscera from the fish with her bare hands.

"I need to get some air. I feel like I'm suffocating," Brenden said. He attempted to lift his body up off of the couch twice before successfully rising to his feet.

"See you in three years," Cecelia muttered, throwing the bloody fish entrails across the room into the trash can. Her anger made her aim bad, and she missed her target. The former insides of the fish hit the white wall above the plastic waste bin, and stuck for a brief moment.

Brenden seemed to grow paler watching the fish guts leave a blood trail on the wall as they slid down into the lidless trash can. He swayed on his feet and his breathing became labored.

"If you pass out, I'm not picking your big ass up. You can lay on the floor all night," Cecelia said, rolling her eyes at her husband's theatrics. He used to hunt and fish all the time. It's how they survived for years when they'd drifted from place to place. He used to skin, gut, and carve all of the kills. Not once had he gotten sick over it.

Brenden walked to the trailer's front door without speaking. He left Cecilia staring at him as he snapped the door shut behind him.

CHAPTER 3

Cecelia thought for sure Brenden would be long gone after she prepared dinner, but he was sitting on the old wooden front deck he had built soon after they moved into the place. He didn't seem to hear her when she opened the door to call him in to eat, and didn't seem to notice the light drizzle that fell on his body, wetting his clothes.

They ate in silence. Brenden fell asleep on the couch after dinner. Cecelia went to her room to sleep. She tossed and turned most of the night, alternating between feelings of bewilderment, rage, and forgiveness.

Something was going on with Brenden, and as angry as she was with him, she was still curious and concerned about her husband. Had he gotten into some bad drugs? Or perhaps he'd suffered a stroke that affected his mind? His personality was mostly the same, but there were a few small differences she picked up on. His squeamishness when she was dressing the fish, his tired movements, the inconsistencies in his story. She called Dr. Hanus the next morning, and an appointment was scheduled for later that week.

As the days went on, Cecelia noticed other odd things about her husband. He drank massive amounts of water and sometimes chocolate milk from the sixty-four-ounce double gulp cup, but she never saw him go to the bathroom. He slurred his words when he spoke, and she accused him of drinking, but he hadn't been anywhere to buy alcohol. She didn't keep any in the trailer. He would sit motionless, staring at nothing, not seeming to breathe, and then suddenly gasp for air. It reminded her of sleep apnea, but he was awake when it happened.

Thursday finally came, and Cecelia drove Brenden across town to Dr. Hanus's office. Dr. Hanus was the only doctor in Kosher Harbor. The town wasn't big enough for a hospital of its own with only a population of three thousand. They sat in the waiting room for over half an hour before they were finally called back to an exam room. A nurse took Brenden's vitals, and told them the doctor would be with them soon. Soon turned out to be another half an hour. Cecelia couldn't keep the simmering anger she was feeling at bay. She always hated waiting, and wouldn't have to be here in the stuffy exam room if it weren't for Brenden.

Finally, Dr. Hanus came in, flashing a smile and showing off his pointy teeth. The man creeped Cecelia out in both appearance and personality. He greeted them, touching her arm and squeezing it. He was very handsy. Cecelia shook his hand off of her arm.

Brenden was a large man. He was tall, six foot and four inches, and easily looked to be over three hundred pounds. However, the nurse recorded his weight as only one-ninety. Dr. Hanus had him step back on the scale to get a more accurate weight, and it did in fact read one-ninety. Assuming the scale was busted, Dr. Hanus weighed himself on it, and when it showed his correct weight, he decided looks were deceiving, and finally accepted that Brenden's weight was one hundred and ninety pounds.

Dr. Hanus examined Brenden, and ordered more tests to be ran at the hospital. He wanted a CT scan and an MRI since Brenden claimed he couldn't remember when he started to have memory loss, and couldn't recall where he had been for the last three years. Blood was drawn, and Brenden swayed and even threw up as it was taken from his body. Dr. Hanus was concerned about how low Brenden's oxygen level was and wrote a prescription for a portable oxygen tank.

The oxygen seemed to help Brenden breathe easier, and he no longer stopped breathing and gasped randomly. The MRI and CT scans showed no injury or disease. His blood tests showed a lower level of red blood cells. A bone marrow test was scheduled to find the cause for the low blood count, but Cecelia considered it to be a waste of time. The red blood cells carry oxygen, and Brenden had low oxygen levels during his exam. He also smoked since before they met. She didn't graduate high school, and didn't have the same education as the doctors and nurses did, but it didn't take a genius to put together that his breathing difficulties were from smoking for most of his life.

These tests were giving her answers, even if they weren't answering anything for Brenden's medical team. Brenden was fine, in the same condition as any other fifty-nine-year-old who lived a rough life. Maybe it was true that he had been off with another woman and now that he was getting older, nobody wanted his ass. He came crawling back to her, to familiarity, and was faking symptoms to avoid explaining himself.

CHAPTER 4

The Claiborne's just returned home from another test, this time an EEG, a brain scan. Dr. Hanus had ordered it, wanting to check for seizures. The scan showed abnormal wave patterns, but none the neurologist could define. Cecelia was annoyed. Kosher Harbor didn't have a hospital in town, and her van was acting up. Driving Brenden back and forth out of town was putting a lot of strain on her and the van.

Brenden sat on the couch, a nasal cannula in his nose delivering oxygen to his body, and stared vacantly in front of him. Cecelia sat at the kitchen table, smoking a cigarette, glaring at her husband. All of the tests, all of the waiting, and all of the results were only pissing her off. Every day that passed, she regretted allowing him back into her life.

"Why don't you just stop it, Brenden?" Cecelia asked.

"Stop what?" Brenden replied.

"This charade. These medical tests aren't showing anything. They're only running up bills. You aren't working and my disability check isn't enough to cover it. I don't even care that you were with another woman anymore. It's the lying that's getting to me now."

Brenden didn't answer her, instead inhaling deeply, and then slowly exhaling.

"Oh, you have to breathe to calm down before talking to me?" Cecelia accused.

"I am calm," Brenden told her.

"Where were you?"

"I told you; I don't know. I don't remember."

"What do you remember?"

"I remember Tonya."

"Tonya? That whore disappeared when you did. Were you with her?" Cecelia demanded. Tonya had moved into the trailer next to theirs. She was always walking around the park in revealing outfits and bikinis. She was young, only in her twenties, and had different men over every night. Cecelia thought she was a filthy slut, and was glad when she left.

"I don't know. I think I was close to her."

"I bet you were," Cecelia muttered, flicking her ash on the kitchen floor.

"Stop being such a jealous bitch," Brenden said. She'd been accusing him for weeks now, and he'd taken it silently until now.

"I'll show you a bitch!" Cecelia yelled, insulted and offended. She jumped to her feet as fast as her damaged knee would allow, and barreled straight to Brenden. She grabbed his portable oxygen tank and heaved it across the room. It hit the window, shattering it, and landed in the yard outside.

Brenden looked up at Cecelia from his spot on the couch. The dull, blank gaze behind his eyes infuriated Cecelia's soul. She wanted a reaction from her husband, but instead Brenden held only a bored look on his pale face.

The tubing that connected the nasal cannula to the oxygen tank was still inside the trailer, hanging on the window sill, and Cecelia grabbed it. She held it in her hands, staring at her husband with wild eyes. She wanted a reaction out of him. She *needed* a reaction.

Standing in front of him, she wrapped the tubing tightly around his neck. Brenden sat motionless, breathing heavily. He didn't lift his arms or do anything else to defend himself as she started to strangle him.

"I'm not backing down, Brenden, not until you tell me the truth!" Cecelia furiously shouted, her own spit flying into Brenden's face. She pulled the rubber tubing tighter around his throat, squeezing and cutting off his air supply. The rope-like tube cut into his skin, disappearing in the folds of his loose neck rolls, and she pulled tighter still. Her only fear was the tube snapping in half as she glared hatefully into her husband's wide-open eyes. Brenden's face turned red and his body began to shake, but still, he made no other movements or sounds.

Cecelia heard her own heavy breathing and felt her heart hammering as she stole the last ounces of life from her husband. Brenden's head slumped forward, and his clenched fists relaxed. Cecelia kept pulling the tubing though, wanting to be absolutely certain he was dead. He could just be unconscious, and she didn't want him to spontaneously recover. She wanted him gone, forever out of her life this time.

Minutes ticked by, one after another, before Cecelia released her hold on the tubing. The muscles in her arms burned from the exertion. Cecelia went back to the kitchen table and sat down. She lit up a new cigarette and took a long drag, letting the menthol sooth her nerves as she continued to glare at her husband's motionless body. There were purple and red lines across Brenden's throat, bruising from the strangulation.

She knew soon she'd have to report his death. When the coroner would see the bruises on his neck she would lie and say he hung himself from the living room ceiling fan. She looked at the dusty fan and wondered if the cheap thing would be able to support his corpse. Cecelia wasn't stupid, but the police in this town were. However, even with as incompetent as the police were, there was a chance they would be able to piece this together rather quickly. She could leave town, but the only money she had come from her disability check. Plus, she was too old and tired to run. After all the years of not having any routine or structure, she craved it now.

Cecelia went to her room and got into bed, leaving her husband's body sitting on the couch in the living room. It was never good to make decisions while emotional, and Cecelia thought it best to sleep before deciding anything. She would think about it in the morning.

CHAPTER 5

Cecelia woke up feeling completely refreshed. It was the best she had slept in ages. The sun was shining brightly through the window curtains and the morning just seemed uplifting. She walked out of her bedroom to find her cigarettes. They were on the table where she always left them. She lit one up, taking a long drag. While smoking, she noticed the window in her living room was broken out.

"How the hell did that happen?" Cecelia asked herself.

She stood up and went to inspect it, and wondered if someone had tried breaking in. She couldn't afford a replacement window right now. She grabbed some duct tape and plastic from the laundry room and placed it over the broken glass. It was already humid outside. The plastic would help keep the coolness the air conditioner provided inside her trailer.

Cecelia dressed and then walked around the block in her trailer park, going to yard sales her neighbors were having. They all introduced themselves and their families as if Cecelia didn't already know them. They invited her to fourth of July cookouts, church gatherings, and neighborhood watch meetings. Cecelia politely declined their invitations, as she always did. These people probably saw her as a lonely old woman, but Cecelia was happy enough being left alone.

Once back home, she sat on the couch, flipped on the tv, and spent the afternoon watching crime shows and chain smoking. Around three in the afternoon, there was a knock on the front door.

Wondering who it could be, Cecelia went to answer the door. When she did, she froze. There stood her husband, Brenden, whom she hadn't seen in three years.

"What the fuck are you doing here?" she asked in shock.

"I've come home to die," Brenden said, opening his arms up.

CHAPTER 6

Brenden looked sick. His skin was pale, his eyes were sunken, his cheeks were drawn. His hair was damp. His breathing was raspy, and Cecelia guessed he had bronchitis. She hoped it wasn't pneumonia. She would need to call Dr. Hanus in the morning.

"Come in," she told him, opening the door wider.

Brenden shuffled inside, and looked around. "It looks the same."

Cecelia stood awkwardly, not knowing what to say. She cried for this man for the last three years, wishing she could have him back, and now here he was.

"Where were you?" she finally asked.

"I can't remember," Brenden answered. He walked to the couch and flopped down hard, his legs giving out from under him.

"What do you mean you can't remember?" Cecelia demanded.

"Just that. I can't remember. It was cold though. Wet. Dark. I know it wasn't a good place. All I knew was I had to come back to you."

"Are you dying? You look like hell."

"I feel like hell," Brenden replied.

"Are you hungry? I can go get some fresh fish," Cecelia offered. She wasn't sure if she believed that he couldn't remember where he was or not, but she didn't want to push it right now. She wanted to feel happy that he was home again, and she wanted to show her affections by cooking for him. Everything else could wait.

"I'm thirsty," Brenden said.

Cecilia got him a cup of water from the double gulp cup she'd saved from the gas station. It was cheaper to refill it than buy new, so she'd kept it to reuse. She was low on chocolate milk and wanted to save the last of it for herself. Brenden drank the entire sixty-four ounces without stopping to take a breath. She assumed he was dehydrated.

"Well, wherever you were, you didn't take good care of yourself," she softly chided him. Cecelia didn't want to risk leaving and this being a dream, so she cooked some salmon she'd bought a few days ago. It still smelled fine, mostly. They ate on the couch together in silence. After eating, Brenden set his plate aside, and his head rested on the back of the couch. He dozed off into a deep sleep.

Cecelia felt tired as well. After rinsing the dishes off in the sink, she went into her bedroom and got into bed. The emotions she felt today were a blur. Happiness, relief, love, and a hint of anger. She fell into a restless sleep.

Cecelia opened her eyes and stared into the darkness. She had an eerie feeling that made her uneasy and turned over. Standing in the doorway, she saw an outline of a shadow, and gasped. She swung her legs over the side of the bed and sat up, reaching for the lamp on her nightstand. Once light filled the room, she saw that Brenden was the one in her doorway. He was staring at her, widely smiling. His arms hung limply at his sides, but his fists were clenched.

"What are you doing, Brenden?" Cecelia demanded, feeling her heart hammering against her chest. Brenden didn't answer. He continued to stare at her. He was still smiling at her for a few more seconds, before he finally turned around and walked out of sight. Cecelia pushed herself up, feeling her knee ache. She needed a replacement, but hadn't heard from the doctor about setting a date yet.

Hearing laughter coming from the living room, she limped through the kitchen, in almost complete darkness. She flipped on the light in the kitchen, and saw Brenden sitting on the couch, drinking water.

"What the hell?" Cecelia asked again.

"What?" Brenden asked, his voice thick. His eyes blinked, adjusting to the light.

"Why were you watching me sleep?"

"I wasn't."

"You were."

"I got up to get some water," Brenden said, his words slurred.

"In the damn dark?"

Brenden just looked at her, not answering. He looked confused.

"Don't piss me off already. I haven't forgiven you yet," Cecelia told him. She saw her cigarettes on the kitchen table, and sat down to light one up.

Brenden lifted the plastic cup to his mouth to finish his water. Cecelia watched him as she smoked. His skin appeared to look gray now, and his hair looked dry, yet greasy at the same time. As Brenden stood up and came into the kitchen to refill his cup, she noticed the smell of sweat mixing in with the odor of smoke. "You need to shower. You smell like death," she said, making a face of disgust.

"My legs feel stiff. Some hot water might loosen them," Brenden agreed. He stood at the sink, drinking the water in his cup until it was empty, and then placed the cup down in the sink. Without another word, he lumbered through the living room and down the hall, to the bathroom at the opposite end of the trailer.

Cecelia heard the water turn on, and she crushed her cigarette out. She continued to sit at the table, listening. She thought she heard low growls coming from the bathroom. She stilled herself, and continued to listen. The growls stopped after a few seconds, and she only heard running water.

Curious, she went to the bathroom and knocked on the door.

"Yeah?" Brenden called out.

"Are you okay in there?" Cecelia asked.

"Yeah."

"Do you need anything? Towels or clean clothes? I think I still have some of your old clothes."

"No."

Cecelia stood outside the door for a few seconds more. Still, she only heard water running.

"Okay, well, I'm going back to bed. Goodnight."

"Night," Brenden called.

Cecelia went back to her room. She shut her door, and moved a chair in front of it. Sitting on the edge of her bed, she held her breath as she listened for any unusual sounds. Hearing none, she dismissed the previous growling sounds as pipes in the old trailer knocking around. Lying down on her mattress, she decided to leave her light on as she slept. Cecelia tossed and turned in her bed like a child, unable to get comfortable.

"Sleep now," She heard a gravelly voice faintly whisper in her ear as she finally crossed the threshold into unconsciousness.

CHAPTER 7

Cecelia felt exhausted when she woke up in the morning. Her bedroom was hot, the July sun warming the aluminum siding of the trailer into uncomfortable temperatures. She made her way to the kitchen to have a cigarette for breakfast. The package of Kools weren't on the table, even though she left them there last night.

"Damn it, Brenden!" Cecelia yelled. Not only had he taken her cigarettes, he had turned off the air conditioner too. The kitchen and living room were just as hot as her bedroom had been. The trailer felt like an oven, slowly baking her alive.

Brenden was asleep on the couch. He was upright, with his head leaning back. Empty cups were scattered on the floor around his feet. He didn't stir as her voice disturbed the quiet.

Cecelia turned the air conditioner on, and grabbed her pack of smokes that sat on the side of the couch next to her husband. The trailer smelled like old meat, so Cecelia went outside to smoke on the front porch. The air outside felt to be a hundred degrees, but it was twenty degrees hotter inside. Nostrils flaring, Cecelia hoped Brenden would roast in his sleep.

She was still pretty angry with Brenden for scaring her. He was acting unusual, and she wondered if he'd suffered a stroke in his absence. Personality changes were common with brain injuries. After the trailer cooled down, she would go back inside to call Dr. Hanus.

Cecelia finished her cigarette, and then went to grab the hose. It hadn't rained in a few weeks, and her flowers and tree could use a drink. In fact, so could she. The water that had been left over in the hose from its last use had warmed under the sun. She sprayed the hot water onto the ground. When it cooled, she used her finger to cover the hose union, spraying the water evenly to hydrate the flowers that surrounded her trailer. She didn't plant them herself. They just appeared every summer, probably planted there from the previous owner. They were pretty, adding some color to the neighborhood, and she left them. Her favorites were the devil's trumpet flowers. They were purple with sharp looking tips.

Once she thought the flowers were drenched enough, she turned the hose onto the Evergreen tree she had planted. She let the water run down the trunk of the tree until it puddled at its base, soaking its roots. Cecelia brought the hose up to her lips to wet her parched mouth. The water filled her mouth, and she tasted wet dirt, sulfur, and something bitter that she couldn't identify. Pine? She spat the water out of her mouth, gagging.

Her first instinct was to blame Brenden for this, but how could he be at fault? He'd just arrived back home. Her second thought was to rush inside and rinse her mouth.

The water from the sink in the kitchen tasted the same, so Cecelia went to the bathroom. That water too had the taste of poisoned earth to it. Instead of using water, Cecelia rinsed her mouth with hydrogen peroxide, and then brushed her teeth with straight baking soda and mouthwash.

When she came out of the bathroom, Cecelia saw Brenden standing at the sink, guzzling the water out of her double gulp cup.

"How can you drink that? It's nasty," Cecelia said.

"Tastes fine to me," Brenden replied, shrugging. He tipped the cup back to his mouth, chugging more water.

"It's probably poisoned. I'm gonna call the maintenance man to check it out. And then we'll call Dr. Hanus to get you checked out too," Cecelia said.

Brenden's appearance changed before her eyes. She no longer saw the old man that he was. Instead, she saw the young man that she'd met when she was fifteen years old. His hair was long, dark, and thick. His body was athletic and toned. He wore the outfit he'd been in the first time they'd met; bell bottom jeans and a patched button up shirt. She sighed, remembering the good times they'd had together.

He turned to face her, still looking like his nineteen-year-old self rather than the fifty-nine-year-old man he was. Cecelia was certain it was her memory playing tricks on her. She was no spring chicken herself, but memories and images didn't move. She shook her head, wondering if the water was indeed poisoned and affecting her vision.

"You're beautiful," Brenden said, dropping the cup into the sink and moving closer to her.

Cecelia put her hand up to stop him. As her palm touched his chest to keep him at a distance, she noticed it looked different. The subtle lines in her hands that showed her age were smoothed. Her fingers looked thinner, less gnarled. The skin was unmarked from age spots.

She realized her knee didn't have the continual dull ache it usually held. Her clothes felt looser on her body. She reached up to feel her hair, feeling a weight on her head. Her braid felt soft, thicker, and longer. She ran her hand down its length, surprised that her hand kept moving further and further. In her older age, she'd kept it shorter, just past her shoulders. She had worn it long, past her waist, when she was younger. Brenden, young Brenden, pulled her into his arms. Cecelia allowed him to hold her. Her mind was reeling, and she was certain she was hallucinating. She'd been on many trips before. Some had scared her, and some had enlightened her. This one just confused her.

Her clothes were what she'd worn when she was younger. Not only could she see them on her body as she looked down at herself, she could feel them. The bellbottoms allowed air to move along her legs. The velvet of her shirt was soft on her skin. She felt pressure from the headband wrapped around her forehead.

For a brief second, she felt content. She felt at peace. All of the anger she felt for Brenden was gone, replaced by his gentle embrace.

An unpleasant scent snaked its way into Cecelia's nostrils. Sulfur. Bitterness. Rotting fish. Rotting fish was a common smell in Kosher Harbor, especially on hot days. Cecelia didn't live in the most affluent part of town, and occasionally bad fish were dumped back into the waters around the bay. But this smell was coming directly from Brenden. Cecelia smelled it coming from his pores as she leaned into him.

She pulled back, gagging for the second time that morning. As she gagged, Brenden's appearance returned to normal, and so did hers. She felt the ache in her knee, and Brenden's eyes became dull again. "What the hell?" Cecelia muttered. The smell disappeared as quickly as it had come, and she was baffled.

"What?" Brenden asked.

"Did you use soap when you showered?" Cecelia asked.

"Yeah."

"Something smells rancid."

"The Hamilton's are probably dumping expired fish," Brenden said. He shuffled back to the couch, and sat down. When he sat, he appeared to be nineteen again.

Cecelia was certain she'd been dosed with something. This hallucination was strong, causing smells, tastes, and feelings she knew weren't real. She picked up the phone to call the maintenance man, telling him to get his ass down to her trailer and check the water. Brenden didn't seem to be affected by whatever drug was lacing their water supply. However, he was acting out of character already, so Cecelia couldn't be sure he wasn't just as high as she was. Her next call was to Dr. Hanus.

CHAPTER 8

Cecelia took Brenden to the doctor, and when Dr. Hanus ordered more tests to be run, she took him out of town to the hospital for scans. Brenden's breathing was labored, and he was given an inhaler. When the inhaler didn't work, he was given a portable oxygen tank.

Cecelia was a homebody, and she hated all of the running around. She hated sitting in the waiting areas of hospitals. Her van was brand new when she bought it, but now fifteen years later, it was barely chugging along. She forced herself to push aside her resentment. Her husband was back home. He was sick, and he needed her care.

Brenden sat on the couch, sucking on his oxygen, and stared at the black screen of the television. Cecelia slipped a pulse oxygen monitor on his finger, and saw the reading was only at eighty-nine percent. She adjusted the oxygen tubing, hoping it would increase his oxygen levels.

He still hadn't told Cecelia where he'd been for the last three years, and she didn't push him. She instinctively knew that he was dying, and she decided to forgive him for everything. She'd be with him, at his side, until the end.

Her nosy neighbors turned out to be helpful and friendly. After they saw Cecelia struggling to help Brenden up the front steps, they came over to help her. Cecelia found a friendship with one of the women named Loretta, who lived across the street.

Loretta was a widow; her own husband had passed away five years prior. Loretta was supportive to Cecelia, bringing her dinner, sitting with Brenden when she needed to run an errand in town, and just lending a listening ear when she needed to talk.

The two of them were sitting outside together, Cecelia drinking a cold pop and Loretta sipping a steaming hot coffee, despite the heat index reaching into the hundreds. It was supposed to rain tonight, and Cecelia was looking forward to a break in the heat.

"Sometimes, he really creeps me out. I catch him staring at me, smiling like a damn fool. I get the sense that he's rotten. Rotten to the core. And I get so angry with him. I want to slap him, and knock that stupid smile off his face," Cecelia whispered.

"I know the feeling too. When my Alfred passed, I felt so angry with him for leaving me. There were nights I wished he was still alive so I could yell at him for leaving me all alone after he died," Loretta said, softly laughing.

Cecelia smiled politely, but she didn't feel the same. Her rage towards Brenden was blinding at times. There were times she'd be sitting at the kitchen table, smoking her cigarette, and would think about throwing it at Brenden's oxygen tank. She smiled thinking about blowing him up. The only thing that stopped her was she didn't want to blow herself up in the process.

She thought about stabbing him when she would prepare dinner sometimes. She thought about smothering him when he dozed off on the couch. She thought about poisoning the food she would prepare for his ungrateful ass. She was sick of him never thanking her for all that she did for him. She didn't know why she wanted to kill him, but something primal from deep inside her bones brought the idea to her mind several times a day.

But then he would start to cough, or gasp for air, or sigh heavily. She would instantly forget the sweltering hate that was boiling up inside of her, and she'd rush over to him. He would hold her hand and look into her eyes, and she felt his love wash over her.

She figured there was probably nothing wrong with fantasizing about killing him sometimes, as long as she didn't act on it.

"I love that man," Cecelia told her friend, and started to cry. Loretta hugged her, as she had done many times before, and tried to offer her neighbor comfort.

The storm rolled in later that evening after it became dark. Thunder boomed and lightning struck a nearby tree, splitting it in half. The outside temperature dropped drastically, and Cecelia was grateful. The wind blew, flapping the plastic that was taped over her living room window.

She made fish for dinner that night, a grouper. It was Brenden's favorite. The air inside the trailer felt stale, and the stench of the fish was lingering in the air. She opened the windows where she could, but the stench only grew.

Brenden sat on the couch, and Cecelia glared at him, assuming he was the cause of the smell. She didn't understand why, but Brenden's skin just reeked. It was as if he'd been saturated in raw sewage. He no longer sweat, but rancid smells still leaked from his pores.

"Go take a damn bath," she told him, lighting a cigarette. She hoped the smell of the smoke would take away from the rotten sewage that was permeating her olfactory sense.

Brenden stood, walking wordlessly down the hall to the bathroom, following his wife's command. Cecelia grabbed a can of air freshener and emptied half the can, spraying it on the couch where Brenden had sat. Satisfied that the smell lessened with Brenden's departure, Cecelia turned the television on to watch her crime show.

A commercial for a car came on, and Cecelia turned the channel to the news. She couldn't afford a new car right now, even though she needed one, and hearing about what she couldn't have would only piss her off. The weatherman was on and he was talking about a hurricane.

"Nothing to be alarmed about for the residents of Kosher Harbor," the weatherman said. "As of now, Hurricane Candi is only a category one and traveling South. She'll miss Kosher Harbor, but we will get a few storms as the storm passes us by."

Cecelia heard rain falling on the metal roof of the trailer, tapping like grains of rice. She heard the wind blowing and thunder rumble. Then she heard growling.

It was a low, guttural, angry sound. The sound of a trapped animal trying to warn off a predator. Cecelia rose to her feet, her knee throbbing. The growls were coming from the bathroom; from her husband.

She moved quietly down the dim hallway and stood outside of the bathroom, listening. The growls became louder. Brenden's throat sounded wet and full of mucus. He sounded evil.

A loud knock at the front door caused Cecelia to jump out of her skin. Her knee twisted from her sudden jump, and she groaned out from the pain. The growls in the bathroom went silent.

Whoever was at the front door banged again, heavily, making the walls vibrate. Cecelia started making her way to the front door. Her knee caused her pace to be slow, and the knocker at the door was getting impatient. The pounding became furiously rapid.

"Hang on a damn minute!" Cecelia yelled, limping her way to the door. She wondered if it was Loretta. She might have locked herself out and was in a hurry to get out of the storm.

Cecelia reached for the door's handle but froze. She heard movement behind her. She spun around, looking down the hall and saw Brenden standing outside the bathroom door. The dim overhead light showed that he was fully naked, and soaking wet. He was smiling at her, his grin goofy and wide, showing rotten teeth. The corners of his eyes wrinkled as his smile grew, spreading wider than humanly possible. He reached towards her with both hands, beckoning her to him, the tips of his fingers black. He started growling behind his smile.

Cecelia's heart raced as she stared at her husband. Her face twisted in disgust as his scent hit her nose. Bile filled her throat and she raised her shirt up to cover her mouth and nose.

The visitor at the door pounded harder, causing their wedding portrait on the wall to fall. Lightning struck, flashing through the windows. For a brief moment, as the bright light penetrated into the shadows, Cecelia saw that her husband didn't look at all like her husband. His nose was missing, hollowed out. The sockets of his eyes were empty. His skin was tanned and leathered, hanging off of his face. His physique was gauntly, as if it had been starved. Once the flash of light faded, the hallway dimmed again. Cecelia was unable to make out the details in his features anymore. However, she continued to see his smile. She took a step backwards.

Brenden's smile fell from his face, and he looked almost disappointed. He dropped his arms, and went back into the bathroom, slamming the door behind him.

Cecelia tried to regulate her breathing. Brenden had done a lot of creepy shit since he'd come back home, but nothing as creepy as that had just been. Her heart continued to hammer against her chest as she tried to calm herself down, still staring at the bathroom door. She was too afraid to move.

The pounding and banging on the front door started up again without warning. Cecelia screamed out loud before opening the door. Nothing could be worse on the other side of the front door than what was behind the bathroom door.

CHAPTER 9

"What do you want?" Cecelia yelled into the night, swinging the door open. A woman stood on the front porch. She was covered in mud from head to toe, wearing something pink that Cecelia couldn't entirely make out due to the thick mixture of dirt and water. Mud caked her hair. It was under her nails, plugging her ears, and even spilling from her mouth. The sight of the woman shocked Cecelia. This had been the last thing she'd been expecting. What in the world was this woman doing out in this storm, let alone on her front porch?

"Brenden," the woman moaned. Her voice rasped as she gagged on the mud that fell from her mouth. She tightly grasped Cecelia's wrist with her hand, mud smearing onto her own skin.

Lightning flashed, and with it came Cecelia's anger. Hearing this woman speak her husband's name created sparks of jealousy that was a thousand times stronger than the bolt of lightning that lit up the sky. It was obvious this woman was here for Brenden, and not in need of any assistance.

"Who are you? His whore?" Cecelia accused, feeling her blood pressure rise. This woman was young, and even covered in mud, Cecelia could tell she was beautiful with her long blonde hair and perfect figure.

"Brenden, please," the woman gasped, holding her stomach as she continued to spit thick mud from her mouth.

"Who in the hell do you think you are? Showing up here trying to take *my* man?" Cecelia yelled, trying to shake the woman's hand off of her wrist. Cecelia had no doubt this was Tonya, the slutty neighbor she assumed her husband ran off with three years ago.

The woman held onto Cecelia's wrist; her grasp still firm. She started to wheeze. The mud was still choking her. It was painfully obvious that she could no longer breathe, but Cecelia didn't care. Brenden had just returned home, and even as creepy as he'd been, she was still glad he'd come home to her, his wife. For better or worse; through sickness and health. This other bitch could hit the road.

"Get your filthy hands off of me," Cecelia yelled, shoving the choking woman away from her.

Her nails scratched Cecelia's wrist as she fell backwards off the front porch. She rolled head over feet down the four steps, and hit the ground. Her neck was bent at an awkward angle and her mouth was wide open, catching the rainwater.

The woman Cecelia assumed to be Tonya laid still, no longer choking; no longer breathing. Cecelia had no intentions of calling for help. The bitch shouldn't have darkened my doorstep. She got what she deserved, Cecelia thought to herself.

"Brenden!" Cecelia screamed, fury coursing through her bones. She dealt with Tonya. Now it was time to deal with Brenden. She walked back inside the trailer, and ran as fast as her knee would carry her down the narrow hallway, to the bathroom.

Cecilia barged though the door. She stood in the doorway, blocking the only way out, and fixed Brenden with a hostile glare. He was soaking in the bathtub, and looked up at her curiously. Her chest rose and fell as she breathed heavily, hearing each inhale and exhale. She reminded herself of a bull. She bared her teeth, struggling to control herself long enough to speak.

"What?" Brenden asked. His face showed concern and worry.

"Why was your whore knocking on my door?" Cecelia asked tightly.

"Who?"

"Who? Who! You know damn well who!" Cecelia screamed at Brenden, rushing across the room and stabbing her finger in Brenden's face. "I'll give you one last chance, Brenden. Tell me where you were the last three years.”

“I can’t remember. I think… I think Tonya was there,” Brenden answered.

“I bet she was,” Cecelia sarcastically replied through clenched teeth.

“She’s cold. I never wanted her to be hurt,” Brenden mused.

“But what about me? To hell with big old Cecelia and her pain, right?” Cecelia bellowed. Something within her snapped as she looked at her husband. She could no longer fight against the urges she’d been feeling for the last weeks.

She suddenly lunged forward, ignoring the protest from her knee, and grabbed Brenden by his hair. She yanked his body forward, pushing his head underwater. Brenden’s arms came up, but he was too weak to fight her away. Cecelia had his body nearly doubled in half, and she put all of her weight on her forearm, which was across the back of his neck. Brenden continued to struggle and tried to push himself up, but Cecelia was stronger and pushed back with more force. She heard the echo of bones breaking as she continued to bend his body and forced him more underwater.

Blood pooled into the bathtub where Brenden's bones poked through his skin from the crushing pressure Cecelia was inflicting. The vertebrae in his spine loosened. One last bubble escaped his lungs and then his struggling stopped.

"You and your tramp can drown together tonight," Cecelia said, laughing maniacally.

Cecilia's body began to hurt and stiffen as she continued to hold him in place. Even though Brenden's body was broken and damaged, Cecelia wanted to be absolutely certain there was no possible chance for resuscitation after she released her hold on him.

After several long minutes, her body could no longer maintain her position. She was too old for this drama. She pushed herself up, and then sat down on the closed toilet, giving herself a moment to recover. Brenden bobbed lifelessly in the shallow bathtub, his body still bent in half and his face in the water. *Good. The dirty dog deserved to die.*

Cecelia left the bathroom, shutting the door behind her. She was tired, and didn't feel like explaining any of this to police or paramedics tonight. She grabbed her cigarettes and went to her bedroom. Sitting on the edge of the bed, she smoked, and thought about what she could tell the police when she woke up in the morning and 'found' the bodies of her husband and his lover.

CHAPTER 10

Cecelia's body hurt. She couldn't remember how she twisted her knee yesterday, but it was certainly throbbing this morning. She would need to call Dr. Hanus and get that son-of-a-bitch moving on scheduling her knee replacement surgery.

She reached for her cigarettes on her nightstand, and saw scratches on her wrist. She couldn't remember how that happened either. Shrugging, she lit the menthol and inhaled the smoke deep into her lungs. After smoking, Cecelia went to the bathroom and showered. She was out of the extra strength Tylenol, so she dressed and then got into her van to go to the pharmacy.

She waved at her neighbor, Loretta, across the street. Loretta stared at her blankly for a moment, as if she didn't recognize who she was, and then smiled kindly, returning a small wave.

Cecelia drove to the pharmacy and picked up several bottles of over-the-counter pain relief medication, and then stopped by the fish market to grab some oysters. She said hello to Sophie, calling her by her first name, as if they were friends, and Sophie gave her the same dumb eyed look Loretta had given her earlier. Sophie started to share a recipe for the oysters that Cecelia had heard a dozen times before. Annoyed, Cecelia didn't give the courtesy of listening, and walked away while Sophie was still talking.

Back home, Cecelia checked her flowers and the Evergreen tree. There had been a storm last night, and she was happy to see that none of them were damaged. It was August, the tail end of summer, but the beginning of hurricane season. It would rain a lot more. Cecelia knew her flowers would stay in bloom for another month or so.

She went inside and started to bake her oysters. She made pasta to go with them, and sat on her couch, eating and watching her favorite crime shows. Her couch seemed to have a faint smell to it that she did not like, but when she got a can of air freshener to spray on it and cover up the smell, the aerosol can was empty.

The time hit three in the afternoon and there was a knock on the door. Cecelia went to answer it, expecting it to be Loretta. She was sure the woman was coming by to give her the rundown on the neighborhood gossip. Instead, she opened the door and froze. It was her husband standing there, arms wide open. She hadn't seen him in three years.

"What the fuck are you doing here?" Cecelia asked, not pleased to see him in the slightest.

"I've come home to die," Brenden answered. A smile formed on the man's face.

CHAPTER 11

"What do you mean you've come home to die?" Cecelia asked, standing in the doorway and glowering at her husband. She was not about to let this rotten dirty dog in without an explanation.

"I'm dying, Cecelia. I need to be with you," Brenden said. He smiled at her again, inviting her into his opened arms.

"You didn't need to be with me for the last three years though, did you?" Cecelia shouted, and slammed the door. She stalked across her small living room and plopped down on the couch.

Grabbing her pack of Kools, she lit one up. She was so angry she was shaking. Just who the hell did that man think he was? She cried for that man for the last three years, and now he wants to come home after he discovered he has an inoperable disease or something?

She sucked in a lungful of smoke to help steady her nerves. She had cried for Brenden for a long time, but life kept moving forward. Cecelia learned how to live without the man she knew since adolescence. Why should he disrupt her life now? She earned her freedom. But here he was, pleading and begging like a dog for her to take him back.

Cecelia stabbed her cigarette out in the overflowing ashtray, and pushed herself up to her feet. She went to the window that had been covered in plastic for longer than she remembered. She wasn't even sure anymore how it had been broken in the first place. It would need to be repaired at some point before winter, but there were bigger fish to fry right now. She peered out the plastic, and saw a blurry image of her husband still standing outside.

He was in the yard, beside the tree. Cecelia loved plants, but wasn't much of a gardener, so she'd bought the Evergreen tree when it was only a foot high and still in a pot. It was fast growing, and was already about seven foot tall. She planted it after Brenden left her.

Cecelia marched to the door. When her hand was on the knob, she stopped. Giving the neighbors a show wasn't what she wanted to do. Her cigarette helped her cool down, but she was starting to feel angry again. Instead of screaming at him, she'd calmly tell him she had to go out and expected him to be gone when she returned.

Mind made up, Cecelia slipped her shoes on, grabbed her purse, and stepped outside into the sweltering heat. Brenden was covered in sweat. His shirt was soaked. Cecelia could smell him, and she made a face of disgust.

"Get a drink from the damn hose," she told him. The last thing she needed was him passing out from a heat stroke in the yard.

Brenden spun around to look at her, and his appearance changed to a much younger version of himself. He wore the clothes she first met him in. Jeans with a flare at the bottom, a patched button up shirt, and bracelets on his wrists. He smiled at her, a crooked smile she could never resist. His hair was shoulder length again and his skin looked healthy. Just as fast as it came, it went away. The young man was replaced with a much older man again. Cecelia blinked, and tried to clear her head. Maybe she was getting dehydrated from the heat.

"I have to go to town. Don't be here when I get back," Cecelia warned, climbing down the stairs of her porch. Her knee was starting to hurt her again, and each step was slow and deliberate. She didn't want to fall down the steps and embarrass herself.

"I need to be home," Brenden told her, coming closer.

Cecelia started walking to her van. Brenden was following behind her, but they were both moving slowly. She wondered how it must look to the neighbors; two people in their fifties chasing after one another, limping along at a snail's pace.

"Go be with your whore."

"You're the only whore for me," Brenden said lightly.

Cecelia could tell his voice was joking and light, meaning to dissuade her, but she was in no mood for jokes. Spinning around, she saw him smiling lovingly at her. This old man's smile didn't look nearly as endearing as it did forty years ago. Cecelia moved closer to him and stabbed her finger in Brenden's chest. "I'm in no mood for your games, Brenden!" she shouted at her husband.

"There's nobody else. There's only you. There's only ever been you," Brenden told her.

Cecelia poked Brenden's chest again, ready to tear into him for lying, but what she felt stopped her. His chest felt squishy. Not just from the fat that he accumulated in age, but as if his bones were softer than they ought to be. "What's wrong with your ribs?" she asked.

"I told you; I'm dying. I've come home to die."

"You're gonna be dead if you're not out of here by the time I get back. I'm not your damn nurse. Go die somewhere else," Cecelia said. She spun around and hefted herself into her van.

Brenden began to make his way over to the water hose while Cecelia struggled to get the van started. The engine finally cranked over after the third try. Cecelia watched as Brenden stood in front of the trailer, in front of her flowers, and began to drink from the hose.

He must have felt her eyes on him because he looked up, and smiled at her again. His smile widened, showing all of his yellowed teeth, and he gave her a small wave. She flipped him the middle finger.

Brenden started to laugh, and Cecelia felt her blood pressure rise. She remembered all the times they would argue before, and how he always found it amusing. He thought if he laughed enough, it would get her laughing too. He thought his laughter would make her see how her anger was misguided. None of this was funny anymore. Not after three years of loneliness, living without him. Three years without seeing his stupid smile. Three years without hearing his obnoxious laugh. Three quiet years of hell, all caused by the man she gave her entire life to.

Cecelia put the van in gear and stomped on the gas pedal. The van lurched forward rather than reversing out of her small driveway, and before she knew what she was doing, she had Brenden pinned between the trailer and her van.

"Cecelia!" he yelled out in pain.

"You shouldn't have come home! I don't want you here anymore!" she screamed back at him, pressing on the gas a little more. The bumper of her van was against his knees, crushing them.

"It's your fault I'm here," he told her, grimacing in pain.

"I'll show you who's at fault," Cecelia said, pushing the gas pedal further. She tried to control her anger but the man brought out the worst in her. All she wanted to do was drive around and give him the chance to leave on his own. She didn't care that he was supposedly dying. He'd hurt her and betrayed her, and she just couldn't forgive that. Then he had the audacity to laugh at her.

Cecelia heard the neighbors yelling, and someone was trying to open her door from the outside. She looked out the driver side window and saw Loretta.

"Stop this! Unlock the door!" Loretta yelled. She was frantically trying to open the door to the van to stop the murder of this man nobody had seen in three years.

"He done me wrong, Loretta," Cecelia told her through the glass.

Loretta's eyes widened, seeing her intentions. She wiggled the handle faster and rapidly knocked on the window, as if that would do anything.

The neighbors were trying to break into the van. One of them was on a cell phone, presumably with the police. A few were trying to help release Brenden. They wouldn't be able to. He was pinned between the trailer and the van, and his knees were already broken. So much for not putting on a show for the neighbors.

The air conditioner in the van didn't work, and it was getting too hot for Cecelia to continue sitting here doing nothing. She was getting more irritated from the smoldering heat than she was the neighbors banging on her windows, trying to break them. Reaching into her purse, Cecelia pulled out her pack of cigarettes and ignited one with a lighter. She inhaled the smoke into her lungs. *Might as well get on with it.*

"I love you," Brenden moaned.

Cecelia slammed her foot down on the gas pedal again, driving it down to the floor. The van jerked forward and she heard the tires spinning in place as it inched forward, making a dent into the side of her home where Brenden's body was crushed into it.

Brenden slumped over onto the hood of her van. A pool of blood started to form under him as he bled out.

Satisfied with his death, Cecelia backed the van up. She finished smoking her cigarette, ignoring the neighbors yelling and crying. She heard sirens in the background, and pulled her lipstick out of her purse. Glancing at Brenden's body lying in a heap in front of her trailer, she was curious why there wasn't as much blood. She expected more. Cecelia applied her lipstick looking in the rearview mirror as she waited for the police to arrive. She wanted to look good for her mugshot.

CHAPTER 12

The bed was hard and the air was stale. The heat in the room woke Cecelia up. She turned over in her bed, and felt like she had a hangover. Her head was spinning and throbbing. She felt tired, more than the usual fatigue she typically felt. She wondered if she had fallen off the wagon last night. Her memory felt fuzzy as she tried to recall what happened. She drew a blank.

She got out of bed and her knee was throbbing, so she went into town to get some Tylenol. She made her way along the coast line to the fish market and stopped by Sophie's stand to buy some oysters. She made oysters and pasta for lunch and watched an episode of her favorite crime show; it was a rerun. She tended to her flowers and Evergreen tree, watering them both with the hose. She made small talk with some of the neighbors about the weather before watching another rerun.

She turned the TV off and decided to take a nap, still unsure of what happened the night before. She tossed and turned, until sleep finally took her. When she woke up, her body felt like she'd been through a meat grinder. Cecelia sat up and swung her legs off the side of her bed. She groaned at the sudden pain that shot through her right knee.

It took more effort than usual to push herself to her feet. When she did stand, she felt a wave of dizziness rush through her body, making her sway unsteadily for a few moments. She still couldn't recall drinking alcohol, or anything else that happened recently. After it passed, Cecelia walked out of her bedroom and into the kitchen. She smoked a cigarette, and then picked up her phone to call her doctor to set up an appointment for her knee pain.

The receptionist who worked for Dr. Hanus scheduled her for the twenty-first of August. It was only the thirteenth. She still had another week of suffering.

Cecelia finished her cigarette and then began to peel an onion. She remembered from her drinking days how eating raw onions had always seemed to help her hangovers. She hoped she was just coming down with a slight cold and hadn't started drinking again. It would be so easy to give in and lose herself in alcohol, but it would be so hard to stop again.

Biting into the onion like it was an apple, Cecelia considered going to an Urgent Care outside of Kosher Harbor. Her knee was really aching this afternoon and it even seemed to be spreading to the other knee. She knew that wasn't possible. It was just her right knee that needed a replacement, but still both knees were killing her.

Cecelia showered and dressed for the day, and when the warm water and pain pill didn't help her feel any better, she decided she would go to the Urgent Care. Maybe they could at least give her stronger pain medicine or recommend her to a different doctor that could schedule her knee replacement surgery quicker. She slipped her shoes on and hobbled outside.

Cecelia saw her beat up van parked crooked in her small driveway, half of it in the grass. The front bumper was dented. Seeing her van confirmed her suspicions. She did drink last night. And apparently, she drove drunk.

"Damn it," Cecelia muttered, inspecting the front bumper. "Wonder what I hit."

She got into the van feeling guilty. She hadn't had a drink in over five years and now her sobriety was shot. She felt so disappointed and angry at herself. However, she didn't feel guilty enough to call the police to ask if there were any hit and run accidents last night. Disability didn't pay enough to afford tickets or higher insurance rates, let alone bail money.

Cecelia checked herself into Urgent Care, and waited for almost an hour before being seen. She hated waiting and sitting next to strangers. The nurse finally called her back, and the exam lasted about fifteen minutes. They told her to get a cane, and gave her a referral to see an orthopedic specialist on August twenty-fifth.

"Thanks for nothing," Cecelia muttered, storming out of the clinic. What a waste of time. At least she didn't have to pay for such a useless appointment; Medicaid took care of her medical bills. But she decided a cane might not be such a bad idea. She picked one up at the pharmacy, back in Kosher Harbor.

Back at home, Cecelia parked her van correctly in the driveway, and used the cane to walk after getting out of the vehicle. It seemed to help relieve some of the pressure on her knee. The hose was lying unrolled in the yard, and she picked it up to water her flowers. When she was watering the flowers, she noticed a large dent in the side of her trailer. So that's what she hit, her own home. She felt better knowing she didn't damage anyone else's property or another person for that matter.

She finished watering the flowers and pointed the hose at the Evergreen tree. She watered the tree and was grateful for its shade. She brought the hose to her mouth and was about to take a drink when she smelled the water. Her face scrunched up in disgust. Cecelia noticed that the water smelled like sulfur.

"Sick," she stated. "That's just sickening." Irritated with the heat and the smells from the water, she tossed the hose down by the tree, and then went to turn the water off.

CHAPTER 13

Cecelia's nap on the couch was disturbed by someone knocking at her door. She opened one eye and glanced at the clock that hung on the wall. It was five minutes after three. She laid down on the couch after having lunch, and had been asleep for over two hours. The nap helped. She no longer felt like she was hung over. The pain in her knee was still there, but to a much lesser extent.

There was another knock on the door.

"Coming," Cecelia called out, pushing herself up into a sitting position. Her cane helped her stand up easier, and then she made her way to the door, opening it.

Brenden stood on the front porch.

"What the fuck are you doing here?" Cecelia asked. He was the last person she ever expected to be on the other side of her door. She thought it would be one of the neighbors trying to invite her to some community event she declined ten times already.

"I've come home to die," Brenden said, opening his arms wide and grinning.

Cecelia stared at him. She wasn't sure how to respond. She was infuriated with him. She had been angry with him for such a long time. But she never stopped loving him.

He didn't seem to have aged much since she last saw him. Still, he was no longer the good-looking man she fell in love with all those years ago. His eyes were the same, even though the skin around them was wrinkled now. His hair was mostly the same, just a little shorter and a couple new patches of gray. For a brief moment, Cecelia saw him as the nineteen-year-old boy she first fell in love with when they first met.

"Come in," she said, stepping back to give him room to enter. Legally, he was still her husband.

Brenden walked inside, and shut the door behind him. "It looks the same," her husband said, looking around the interior of the trailer.

Cecelia watched him take in the environment, and then his gaze met hers. They looked at each other in silence for a few moments, and again Cecelia saw the man she loved. She began to hysterically sob, and fell into his arms. Her husband had come back to her.

CHAPTER 14

Brenden couldn't explain to Cecelia where he'd been. He claimed he couldn't remember. Cecelia wasn't sure if he was telling her the truth or faking amnesia. However, she herself couldn't even remember last night.

He couldn't explain to her why he said he had come home to die. She wondered if he had been diagnosed with something, some devastating news, and turned to alcohol. Before they decided to become sober, Brenden was a heavy drinker. It didn't seem likely, but maybe he drank every day for the last three years, and drank enough to black out every single time, unable to remember.

Or it was possible his illness was due to a traumatic brain injury. He could have had a stroke, or dementia. Whatever the cause, he knew to come back home. She would make him an appointment with Dr. Hanus to get him checked out.

Cecelia went to Sophie's Seafood Sensations and purchased a trout. Sophie seemed surprised when Cecelia greeted her by first name, as if they were longtime friends, but she smiled kindly and said hello anyway. Cecelia listened politely as she was given a recipe suggestion for the trout. It was one she heard the old woman tell her a hundred times by now, but she remained patient and let Sophie feel useful. Poor old dear would probably end up in a home soon. Cecelia wondered if she acted this way with all her customers.

Brenden was asleep on the couch when she returned home. He was sitting upright, with his head back. He was silent, and Cecelia became worried. She didn't see his chest rising and falling as he slept.

She urgently walked over to him, and jumped when he suddenly gasped for air. She ended up twisting her bad knee from the scare. This caused the ache in her knee to flare up, and she regretted not walking with her cane.

Cecelia prepared the trout the way Sophie suggested, and Brenden and her ate in the living room, watching TV together. If it wasn't for Brenden asking for massive amounts of the sulfur smelling water, it would have felt as if the last three years without him never happened at all.

Cecelia was able to get Brenden in to see Dr. Hanus the next day. She felt jealous that he was able to get in so quickly, but when she called for herself, she had to wait. Dr. Hanus was curious about Brenden's condition, and ordered several tests. Over the next few days, Cecelia drove Brenden out of town to the hospital and specialists. He had CT scans, MRI scans, X-Rays, and blood work. It was a lot of waiting, a lot of driving, and a lot of frustration. Brenden was given oxygen, and that irritated her. She was glad that it helped him breathe easier, but she was annoyed she would have to smoke outside now.

Brenden had a brain scan, and his brain wave patterns made the neurologist get excited. "We usually see these patterns in patients that are in a vegetative state. It's very obvious you are not in a vegetative state," the doctor told Brenden.

"No, can't say that I am. But I do feel like a potato, past my prime," Brenden said, and coughed.

"I'm going to consult with some of my colleagues about these scans, and we may want to run further tests again."

"Is it possible your machine is messed up?" Cecelia asked.

"That is always a possibility, but I doubt it. Your husband is a special case, Mrs. Claiborne."

Cecelia and Brenden left the hospital with more appointments set up. During the walk across the parking lot to their van, Brenden started to wheeze, and they had to stop so he could catch his breath. He leaned against a random van in the parking lot. It was a much nicer van than her own; a newer model, clean, and there were no dents in this one.

August twenty-first arrived, and Cecelia left Brenden at home on the couch to go to her own appointment with Dr. Hanus. He informed her that she'd need to lose forty pounds in order to have her knee replaced, and wrote her a prescription for a much stronger opioid for her pain. While she was there, she spoke with Dr. Hanus about getting Brenden a motorized wheelchair. There was a lot of walking when they went out of town for Brenden's appointments. The hospitals and specialists outside of Kosher Harbor were in large buildings that had even larger parking areas. It was hard for him, and Cecelia wanted to make things as easy as she could. Dr. Hanus listened, and agreed that a scooter would be medically necessary for Brenden.

Brenden could walk around the trailer easily enough, so Cecelia didn't need to hire anyone to build a ramp to help him get inside. That was a good thing, because any extra money from her disability check was already going towards Brenden's appointments. She got assistance to get him signed up on Medicaid, but she still had to pay for gasoline to drive him around. Her old van wasn't running the best these days and could use a tune up itself.

The scooter was delivered, and it made their lives easier. That's all Cecelia wanted to do, make things easier for the man she loved; a love that would never die.

CHAPTER 15

Cecelia found it surprising that spending time with her estranged husband seemed natural and unforced. She always imagined if he ever did come back home, she would be furious with him. Their relationship seemed natural, as if he never left her in the first place. But she did become annoyed quite frequently with him. It was a lot of work running him around, but Cecelia was glad that he was home. He still couldn't explain his absence, but it didn't matter. What mattered was he was back where he belonged. With her.

Brenden continued to sleep on the couch rather than in the bedroom with her. He breathed easier in an upright position, and it was closer to the kitchen sink. He drank gallons of water each day. Cecelia had to go to the gas station and buy fountain pop to get more of the sixty-four-ounce double gulp cups Brenden preferred to drink from. He drank without pausing to breathe, and Cecelia worried about his oxygen levels. He would gulp the water down until he was so waterlogged that he could no longer move, and then pass out for a short nap.

Cecelia offered to fix up the spare bedroom for him. She hadn't been in there in years. Even before Brenden left, they had no use for that room. She offered to get him a hospital bed so he could raise it and adjust it to his liking while his body was spread out, but he declined. He said the couch was just fine. Still, Cecelia had Dr. Hanus write out an order for a hospital bed. It would be delivered soon.

Cecelia slept alone in her bed, and Brenden stayed on the couch. She didn't mind his preference not to sleep with her. She liked having the extra space. Brenden would cough and gasp while he slept, and that would have kept her awake. She could sleep more peacefully by herself.

It was the middle of the night, and Cecelia was slowly roused from her sleep as her bladder sent signals to her brain, indicating it was full. She was irritated (so many things in her life irritated her these days) and she tried to ignore it. Fighting against the urge seemed to wake her up even more, and she started craving a cigarette. She decided to just get up and give in to her body's demands, have her smoke to relax again, and then come back to bed.

Turning over, she noticed someone kneeling down at her bedside. Her anger disappeared and was replaced with an instant fear. Her blood ran cold as the skeletal face in the shadows stared at her. The hairs on her arms stood on end, and she blindly reached out for her cane.

"Oh!" Cecelia gasped, jostling out from the covers as fast as her body could move, and up against the wall. She was trapped. The grotesque skeleton, covered in decaying flesh, who was in front of her smiled. The boney skull was covered in a thin layer of decaying skin; its lips still intact. It had short hair that was matted down with mud. Its white teeth glowed, reflecting from the moonlight that slid in from between the cracks of her curtains. The thing's head started to move closer to her, its smile growing wider. Its breath smelled awful. It breathed heavily as it moved; smells of sulfur, ammonia, old fish, and decay spewed from its mouth. The undead creature's face inched forward as it climbed onto the bed with Cecelia. Clumps of rotted skin and intestine fell from the skeleton as it crawled closer to her, inch by inch. It was inches from her face before the thing closed its eyes and puckered its lips. She instinctively knew that it was leaning in for a kiss.

Still trapped between the wall and the monster on her bed, Cecelia's hand finally found her cane at the foot of her bed. She raised it and swung it down. The metal connected solidly against the top of the skull. It fell face first into the mattress, and then crawled in reverse as it disappeared off the bed into the darkness.

Cecelia jumped off the bed, her body moving faster than normal. She flipped the light switch on to see the intruder in her bedroom. Nobody was lying on the floor beside the bed. She gripped her fingers around her cane and tried to bend over to get a closer look under the bed, from a distance. She didn't see anything under the bed. It was completely empty.

It couldn't have been a nightmare, Cecelia thought to herself. The experience felt so real to her. She felt her cane connect with the intruder's skull. She still had the wicked smile of the monster's face in her memory. She remembered the rancid smell of its breath. Yet, there was nobody else in her room. The bedroom wasn't that big. There weren't many hiding places. She never kept items under her bed, because her body wasn't able to get up and down like it used to. Holding her cane like a bat, Cecelia walked to her closet. Bracing herself, she pulled the door open, ready to swing. There were only her clothes and a laundry basket in the small closet. She used the cane to move her clothes from side to side, searching for the intruder. There was no one. The bathroom door in her bedroom was already open and she peeked inside. She looked the bathroom over slowly, not wanting to miss anything. The tub was empty, the glass shower door showed no one hiding on the other side. She went to the sink and opened the cabinet door underneath it. Nothing but folded towels.

Cecelia lowered her cane. Maybe it had been a nightmare after all. She gave up searching, closed the bathroom door, and looked at her bed again. She gasped. There, on her white bedsheet was a muddy face print. Cecelia quickly left her bedroom and went to check on Brenden. She considered he might of be messing with her. He always found it funny when she was riled up. She would kill him if it turned out to be her husband playing some sick joke on her in the middle of the night.

Brenden was sound asleep on the couch, and his face was dry and clean. There was no way for him to move out of her room, clean up his face, and get into position on the couch in the amount of time it took her to look in her closet and bathroom. He moves just as slow as she does. Besides that, she went to sleep with her bedroom door closed, and she didn't hear it open or shut.

Was it possible the face imprint on her bed was from her own face? She went into the bathroom at the end of the hallway to look at herself in the mirror. Her face was clean, but it was different. It was forty years younger. And it wasn't just her face that was different. Her black hair was long, reaching down below her waist. Her skin was smooth. She reached a hand up to touch her face, and saw her hands were younger and girlish in the mirror's reflection. Her fingernails were painted a dark cherry red, the color of blood.

Standing behind her, Brenden's reflection appeared. He was forty years younger too, and he rested his hand on her shoulder. She felt his touch, and leaned back against his body, staring at who they used to be. Who they still were, even if their physical looks had changed. Brenden wrapped his arms around her.

She felt her heartbeat slow as she relaxed in his embrace, and she sighed. She had a nightmare earlier, and that's all it was. She felt warm and safe here, Brenden's arms wrapped around her, and nothing could replace that feeling. They weren't teenagers anymore, Cecelia knew that. But that's how she always thought of them when they were together, as two teenagers that were madly in love with one another.

Cecelia turned around to return the hug, but instead of seeing the man she knew, she found herself standing face to face with the undead creature from her bedroom. Its skin was peeling off, hanging from its face. Its eyes were dry and deflated. The lips were thinned and dry. Its hair was wet with mud and clumps of hair was missing altogether. The room was filled with a horrible odor.

Cecelia tried to take a step back, but was held tightly by the boney fingers. She looked down and saw the shirt it was wearing had holes in it and was covered in blood. The rotting corpse squeezed her arms as she continued trying to escape.

Cecelia had never been a push over. She was a fighter, and so she began to fight against the grip this thing, this monster, had on her. She put both of her hands on its right arm to pry it off of her, and felt the flesh tear away from its forearm. Cecelia gagged at the frightful scene, as the smell in the room grew stronger. Putrefied rot.

Startled and trembling, she released her grip on its arm and wrung her hands. She felt chunks of moist, decaying skin on her hands and looked at them in horror. There was no blood, but instead a sludgy black substance that covered her hand. Her stomach turned and she was certain she was going to throw up.

This thing, a gruesome monster, that pretended to be Brenden in the mirror, still had a hold of her and was pushing closer into her. Cecelia's eyes moved away from her hands and back up to its disfigured face. It was leaning in to kiss her. She was trapped against the sink and she screamed out in fear. Her mouth was wide open as she screamed for her life, and the walking corpse planted its lips on Cecelia's. Tears rolled down her cheeks as the creature started to moan in pleasure as its lips pressed into hers. Its tongue penetrated her mouth, and licked the backside of her teeth. The stench was revolting.

She was sick with fear, but she knew she had to suck it up to get herself out of this situation. When it came to fight or flight, Cecelia always chose to fight. Snapped out of her stupor, Cecelia again grabbed at its arm. This time she ignored the squelches and tearing as she tightened her grip, and then yanked.

A low cry escaped from her mouth when their lips separated. She ripped the thing's arm completely off of its body. She was still being held by one hand, but she could move more freely. She was not going to let that rotten face kiss her again, and spun around, putting her back against the monster.

In the mirror, she saw their reflections again. Her and Brenden. Brenden leaned over her and kissed her neck, and she felt his dry lips pressing against her skin.

Seeing Brenden's reflection was easier to fight against. She slammed her body backwards against who, or whatever, was pressing up on her.

Their bodies collided with the wall, and she ran out of the bathroom, her knee pain stabbing at her, and headed for the front door. In the living room, Brenden was still asleep on the couch.

CHAPTER 16

Cecelia ran out of the trailer, grabbing her keys off the hook by the door along the way. She didn't even bother yelling to wake Brenden. She got in her van, locked the doors, and tried to still her breathing. Looking down at her hands, she saw they were still covered in black sludge, and she started gagging again. She opened her dash and grabbed a handful of napkins to wipe her hands on. Sweat poured down her face, and she felt suffocated by the van's hot interior. She needed fresh air, but was terrified to roll the windows down.

Deciding it would be safe to lower them while she was moving, Cecelia turned the key in the ignition and the van roared to life. She backed out of her driveway and started driving around before manually cranking the window down. The air felt refreshing as it hit her face, allowing her to breathe easy again.

Cecelia didn't know how to explain what she just experienced, other than to assume she was delirious from lack of sleep. But she *had* been sleeping just fine since Brenden came back home. Maybe that was part of it. Maybe it was the stress getting to her. He suddenly come home after three years of nothing, and she was forced to run him to a ton of appointments. She had her own physical pain to deal with, but had been ignoring her mental pain.

She pulled into a gas station, and grabbed a dozen paper towels that were at a window washing station. She scrubbed at her hands again, trying to clean the rest of the black goo off of her fingers and steering wheel.

Out of the corner of her eye, Cecelia caught sight of a woman stapling a piece of paper onto a wooden post near the entrance of the gas station. The woman wore a purple turban with a gold cross-stitch pattern. Curly brown locks of hair stuck out from the bottom from its bottom. Her wrist and neck were decorated in heavy jewels. Cecelia recognized the woman. It was Celeste, Kosher Harbor's onc-and-only psychic.

Three years ago, after Brenden first left her, Cecelia went to see her. Celeste had a small palm reading business called The Red Hand, down the road from the church, and Cecelia had been desperate for answers.

"You will be forgotten," Celeste had told her, holding the tip of her ring finger as her eyes grew big.

"Brenden won't forget me. He'll come back. I just want to know where the hell he went," Cecelia demanded.

"Do not worry, he isn't alone. After all, home is where the heart is," Celeste replied.

Cecelia stormed out. The woman's cryptic answers enraged her. She wanted answers, not riddles. She felt stupid being scammed out of fifty dollars, and kicked over a potted plant on her way out.

Seeing the woman now, Cecelia decided she was still owed part of the session. She paid fifty dollars after all, and that was a lot of money for someone on a fixed income. Brenden *was* home now. Perhaps the woman wasn't as kooky as Cecelia thought, and just had her words mixed up.

"Hello, it's me, Cecelia," she said, approaching the psychic.

Celeste turned and look at her. "Hurricane Candi is coming," the woman predicted.

Cecelia was going to ask about Brenden, but then didn't speak. Celeste looked wild eyed and near possessed. "That hurricane isn't coming this way. It's heading South. Besides, it's only a category one."

"Wrong. Wrong! It's going to make a turn, and it's going to grow. It's going to kill."

She was starting to regret crossing the parking lot to talk to this woman. She didn't want to talk about the weather. This lady was crazy three years ago, and she was even crazier now.

"Mark my words," Celeste warned, reaching her hands up to the sky. "It will hit home."

"I think I'll trust the weatherman," Cecelia said, turning around to leave. Now wouldn't be the right time to ask anything about Brenden. This woman was clinically insane.

"Three days from now," Celeste yelled into the quiet night. She had her eyes closed now and was spinning in circles, still looking up to the stars.

"Crazy bitch," Cecelia muttered, making her way to the gas station doors. She purchased herself a pack of cigarettes and a new lighter. In her haste to get out of the trailer, she forgot to grab them off the kitchen table. She also didn't use the bathroom, and that's what woke her up in the first place. She asked the cashier for the key to the ladies' room. She refused to look in the mirror.

Cecelia continued to drive around until the sun began to rise, and then finally went home. Things would probably be safer with the sun up. Brenden was still on the couch when she walked in, and woke up at her arrival.

"Can you get me some water?" he asked, licking his lips. Cecelia shuddered remembering the dry lips of her night time visitor.

His eyes fell closed again, and Cecelia studied him. If she stared at him long enough, he might just crack and admit to playing a horrible practical joke on her last night. Instead, he just remained still and silent, seemingly unaware she was fixing him with a look.

"Get your own damn water," Cecelia snapped, surprising herself. She wasn't sure why she felt anger towards Brenden. She didn't sleep though, and figured it was due to sleeplessness. "I'm sorry. I'm tired. I'll get your water."

She went to the kitchen and filled two of the double gulp cups for him, knowing he would want more than one. Holding the plastic cup in her hand, she regretted not getting herself a cold pop when she was at the gas station. Cecelia didn't drink coffee, and she would need a caffeine boost today. She watched as Brenden drank the water, and gave him a refill in both cups when he asked. She also made him a bowl of cereal and had one herself.

As Brenden chugged the fourth cup of water, Cecelia finally became aware of something. She was only thinking about it now because the entire reason she woke up earlier was her need to use the bathroom. Brenden drank so much water, yet she never saw him go to the bathroom. How had she missed that? He would shower when she insisted, but she never heard him flush the toilet, but never has he went to the bathroom on his own.

And why wasn't he asking her where she'd been all night? If he had left in the middle of the night and came home hours later, she would be furious. Of course, he had been gone for three years, so he had no right to question her about being gone for a few hours.

Feeling braver with the sun up, Cecelia walked down the hall to the bathroom. She looked inside, and saw no rotted body parts lying on the floor. In the mirror, she saw the reflection of her fifty-five-year-old self.

Everything must have been a vivid nightmare, probably left over fragments and remnants from all of the drugs and alcohol she took over the course of her life. She walked to the opposite end of the trailer, to her bedroom and looked inside. Just as she remembered from the night before, a muddy faceprint was still smeared on her white bedsheet.

CHAPTER 17

The clouds in the sky were dark and hanging lower than normal, putting the town on full alert. Perhaps Celeste, the town's psychic, wasn't as crazy as Cecelia thought she was. Hurricane Candi had grown in size and power at an alarming rate. What was even worse, the storm shifted, making a dramatic turn, and was headed directly for Kosher Harbor. No one saw it coming. No one was prepared.

There was little Cecelia could do to prepare. She lived in a mobile home, and there was sure to be damage. She was thankful the trailer park wasn't too close to the ocean, so at least she wouldn't have to worry about significant water surges flipping her trailer over. There would definitely be some flooding, but she hoped it wouldn't be too overwhelming. She was more worried about the powerful winds.

Cecelia tried to buy as much supplies as she could afford, but the stores were packed and in chaos. At the next store she stopped at, she gave up trying to be nice, and started pushing and shoving everyone. She didn't care what others needed. She grabbed a case of bottled water, using it to shove others out of her way, and left without even bothering to pay for it.

The storm came, and it *was* a bad one. The plastic that covered her window ripped away, and rain poured inside on her carpet. The power went out all across Kosher Harbor, and the wind rocked the trailer so hard Cecelia was afraid that it would surely tip over. The tropical storm created several tornadoes, and the sounds the storms produced were terrifying. The storm surge came, flooding Kosher

Harbor. Cecelia could see the water rushing on the ground, and again she was thankful that she wasn't close to the ocean. Her trailer would have been swept away.

Hurricane Candi lasted for a week. Homes were destroyed. Several hundred lives were lost. The Evergreen tree Cecelia planted three years prior was ripped from the ground and a large branch from the tree had impaled itself through the trailer's roof. A neighbor's metal fence post stuck out of the hood of her van. The tiny shed that housed Brenden's motorized scooter was decimated. His scooter was turned upside down, leaning against the trailer Tonya had once lived in. But she and Brenden were still alive. Besides the gigantic limb that penetrated through the hallway roof to the floor in her trailer, her home was still a home.

When the water receded enough for people to go outside, Cecelia's neighbors started organizing a neighborhood clean-up. They came to her door and offered to remove the tree for her once they finished helping another neighbor. Cecelia reluctantly agreed after taking a dozen photos with her digital camera for the insurance company. She didn't want to help clean up other people's property, but she knew that she wouldn't be able to move the tree herself. She couldn't afford to pay anyone to move it, and Brenden certainly couldn't do it.

During the week of the storm, her husband had gotten worse. His breathing was more labored, and he seemed to grow sicker. He kept asking for water, but Cecelia told him they needed to ration it. He was acting if his body would dry out by lack of water intake.

Cecelia told her neighbors she needed to take care of Brenden today, but she would be able to help them out tomorrow morning. Her hope was that they would get the tree cleaned up for her later tonight and throw tarps over her roof where the branch speared its way through.

Brenden was much weaker, and she helped him settle onto the couch. She propped pillows behind him and turned his oxygen up. He was struggling to stay awake. Once she was certain he was comfortable, she grabbed her cigarettes and stepped outside to smoke.

She carefully walked around her yard, inspecting the damage. The skirting around her trailer, and most of all her neighbor's, had been blown off and would need to be replaced. She could see cinder blocks and pipes underneath, and was amazed that the trailer was still standing after enduring such violent winds.

Her flowers were gone. She hoped the plants would come back next season. It was unfortunate that her tree had fallen. That wouldn't be so easily replaced. She was proud of that little tree. She walked over to the fallen tree, and saw that it had been ripped out of the ground, roots and all.

She noticed something that didn't make sense to her, and walked closer to the hole that the tree had left in her yard. She peered inside of the ground, and gasped. Lying under dirt and wood debris was a muddy skeleton. Desiccated skin that looked like brittle leather covered the skeleton, stretching over the bones. The skeleton was dressed, wearing a ripped flannel shirt and jeans. Its hair was caked down with mud. The eyes were empty sockets. They reminded her of someone. The skeleton in the hole was Brenden. And beside him was another skeleton. This one wore a grimy pink night dress, and had wisps of blonde hair. Tonya, the whore neighbor. And Cecelia remembered she was the one who put them there.

CHAPTER 18

FLASHBACK

THREE YEARS AGO

"What the fuck are you doing here?" Cecelia demanded, staring at her good for nothing husband.

He stood on the front porch, clearly hung over. "I want to come home. This is where I belong; home with you. I've come home."

"You're gonna come home to die if you don't get off my front porch! This isn't your damn home anymore, Brenden. Go back to your little floozy."

"I made a mistake, Cecelia. I was stupid, and I didn't plan this. I didn't mean to hurt you. I never meant to hurt you. I just had a moment of weakness."

Three days ago, Cecelia had caught Brenden laying on the living room couch with Tonya on top of him. She never felt so angry or betrayed in her entire life. She screamed in sheer rage, and grabbed Tonya by the hair of her head. Cecelia dragged her out onto the porch and threw her down the steps.

Before this, Cecelia had never been a violent person. She never hit anyone before. She never even raised her voice at another person before. But catching her husband with another woman made her snap. Something woke up inside Cecelia; something evil.

Cecelia turned her wrath to her husband. She felt the insulation on the wires of her brain melt away, and she pounded her fists against Brenden's chest. She couldn't see. The rage had turned her vision red. She banished him from their home. She wouldn't allow him to gather any of his belongings.

She told him if he ever came back, he would regret it.

And now here he was. She warned him. "Fine. Come in," Cecelia told him. Her voice was eerily calm, and Brenden relaxed.

He walked inside, and looked around. Cecelia closed the door. "It looks the same. I thought for sure you'd tear my shit up," Brenden said. His eyes fell on the entertainment stand that he built a few years back. He looked at the pictures of him and Cecelia that hung on the walls. His favorite lap blanket was still resting on the brown couch.

"I've been too busy being upset about my cheating dog of a husband to do any damn redecorating," Cecelia snapped, walking into the kitchen. Her cigarettes were on the table, just under their wedding portrait. She glanced at the photo but ignored the pack of Kools. Her eyes were on another object.

Brenden sat down on the couch, and kicked his shoes off. It felt so good to be back home. His three-day affair with Tonya had been a mistake. It wasn't even about her. He never had eyes for her. The only woman he ever looked at was his wife.

Tonya paid him twenty dollars each week to mow her yard. She didn't know how to use a lawnmower, and twenty bucks was twenty bucks, so he agreed to the job. One day, it had been hot and she offered him a cold beer when he finished. He accepted. It was impulsive and stupid. It was so hot outside, and the cool condensation on the can felt good against his skin. Before he knew what he was doing, he had chugged it.

Then she offered him a second, and a third. Within minutes, they were both drunk and laughing together. He never meant to sleep with Tonya, it just happened. And he regretted it more than anything in the world.

"Thanks for letting me back in. Can we sit down and talk about this?" Brenden said, already sitting down. "I want to spend the rest of my life making this up to you," Brenden said.

Cecelia walked over to stand in front of Brenden, one hand behind her back. "Till death do us part," Cecelia replied. She brought the butcher knife out from behind her back and stabbed it into Brenden's chest. She pulled it out, and thrust it back in, again, again, and again.

Brenden gasped as the knife sliced into his body, puncturing his lungs. Metal slicing into skin was painful in its own, but the feeling of suffocating was worse. He stared at his beautiful wife and watched her face become stained with his own blood.

"You good for nothing, cheating, son-of-a-bitch!" Cecelia screamed at him as she continued to stab him. She stabbed him thirty-seven times; the same number of years they had been married. She dropped the knife at Brenden's feet. His body was still.

She went outside to the small shed and grabbed a shovel. She started to dig. Her mind was racing. Time had no meaning anymore. All that mattered was digging this hole. And so, she continued to dig until it was done. She wasn't sure how much time had passed. She didn't care. It was still dark out, but she was sure the sun would show its face sometime soon.

"Cecelia?" a voice called out, startling her.

Cecelia spun around, shovel in hand. It was Tonya, the other woman. She was dressed in a frilly pink nighty that left nothing to the imagination. "What do you want? Can't you see I'm busy?"

"I heard a noise outside and it woke me up. What are you digging a hole for? And at this hour?" Tonya asked, walking closer.

"I'm planting a tree later today. Hey, since you're here, do you mind helping me with something inside really quick?"

"Oh, sure. I was hoping to talk to you anyway, I wanted to apologize for the other day. You know, with Brenden."

The two women started walking to the front porch, Cecelia falling behind Tonya. Tonya continued to talk about how sorry she was and she hoped they could move past it all.

Cecelia swung the shovel as hard as she could into the back of Tonya's head. Her neighbor went down hard. Cecelia stepped closer, but Tonya rolled over and kicked Cecelia in her right knee. Something popped and Cecelia fell onto Tonya. The two women hit and scratched at one another until Cecelia wrapped both hands around Tonya's neck. She pushed down and squeezed as hard as she could, choking the woman who tried to steal her man. Tonya struggled to break free but was no match for the woman with a broken heart. She pressed both thumbs down into her neck as hard as she could until Tonya stopped struggling.

"Brenden belongs to me. He will never leave me again," Cecelia whispered to Tonya's lifeless body. She grabbed her neighbor by her blonde hair and drug her to the fresh hole. She pushed her limp body over its edge and it hit the bottom with a thud.

Cecelia went back into her trailer and lit up a cigarette. She sat on the couch beside her dead husband and blew smoke into his face. "I warned you not to come back here," she told him. He didn't respond. After she finished smoking, she grabbed

Brenden by his arms and started to drag him out the front door and down the steps.

The adrenaline rush was still strong and she was able to drag him to the hole with ease. Cecelia didn't hesitate. She shoved Brenden and his body fell on top of Tonya's. Cecelia walked back to the porch to grab the shovel. She made use of it, filling the hole back in with dirt. She decided to keep her word and plant a tree today. She would also have to rent a carpet cleaner.

CHAPTER 19

Cecelia went back inside her trailer, the two skeletons still fresh in her mind. Brenden was still asleep on the couch. But Brenden was dead. She killed him. She forgot she did, but seeing their skeletons, she remembered now.

If he's dead, who is asleep on my couch? "Wake up," Cecelia ordered.

Brenden began to stir, and Cecelia poured three water bottles into the big gulp cup for him. He sucked them down, one after the other.

Cecelia grabbed a cigarette and lit it. She inhaled. "Who are you?" she asked after he finished the last of the water. His skin seemed to recover as he drank the water. His face no longer looked dehydrated and drawn. It became smooth and had an even tone. Cecelia shuddered. She hadn't realized that effect before.

"I'm your husband," Brenden replied.

"I killed you."

"Yeah," was all he said.

"Your body is buried in the yard. I planted that tree on top of you two," Cecelia said in disbelief.

"That's where you put us?"

"Why are you… here?"

"I come home to die. It's what I do. It's the last thing we did. It's the last thing we'll ever do."

"Am I dead too? Is this Hell?"

"This is Kosher Harbor."

"Am I dead?" Cecelia demanded.

"You're alive."

"But you're dead."

"I think so. I'm certainly not alive," Brenden noted.

"Why now? Why three years later?"

"I've been back before now. This isn't the first time. You kill me, and then I come back. Don't you remember?"

"No, I don't. What the hell? I took you to doctors! I saw them take your blood. I saw them do tests."

"I don't know how it works. I'm just grateful for the time I get to spend with you. I've always wanted to make things right between us," Brenden uttered. His respirations started to increase, and Cecelia moved closer to adjust his oxygen tank.

She felt dizzy, adjusting the oxygen for a dead man. "What if I don't kill you? Does this stop?" she asked. She didn't understand what was happening. None of it made any sense to her. She just wanted her normal life back.

"I'm already dead. I can't keep living. I'll die anyway. The longer I'm back, the stronger the curse becomes. You see things, horrible things, that aren't real. And then you finally snap and kill me.

"Why didn't you tell me this before?"

"I don't remember right away. It's fuzzy when I first come back. And when I finally do remember, I just want to forget. I've tried telling you but you never believe me, and my deaths become a lot more violent if I do tell you. You've been killing me for three years now."

"Were you haunting me? Late at night, when I would see shit, was that you?" Cecelia asked, suddenly feeling irrationally angry.

"I'm not even me. So, I don't know what the thing is that haunts you. I think it's an echo of myself, just like I am. I don't know how this works. I think it has something to do with the last time we got high together. We felt spiritually connected that night, remember? It was our first night in Kosher Harbor; at the cemetery."

CHAPTER 20

Cecelia remembered everything now. She remembered the warning the sketchy stranger gave them when they traded goods when they first arrived in Kosher Harbor. He told them it would change them forever. She remembered seeing Celeste after Brenden left her, telling her she would be forgotten. She remembered Sophie never seeming to recognize her. Loretta looking at her like she was a stranger. The damn annoying neighbors repeatedly asking her to join them in activities after she'd hatefully slam the door in their faces.

Celeste was right. Every time she killed Brenden, everyone within Kosher Harbor forgot her. Even Dr. Hanus. That's why her knee replacement kept getting put off or rescheduled. Did the medical files disappear just like their memories?

Brenden looked up to his wife, sitting beside him on the couch. Their eyes connected and Brenden smiled his crooked smile. "I love you, Cecelia," he said.

"I love you too, Brenden," she replied. They both closed their eyes as she leaned in and gave him a kiss. Brenden's eyes did not open again. He seemed peaceful and content. She wasn't sure what to do. Did she call for an ambulance? Would it make a difference? They were too busy searching for bodies from Hurricane Candi. She decided not to call anyone. Besides, Cecelia had two skeletons buried in her yard that she needed to take care of before summoning anyone. Everything was so far-fetched that she couldn't wrap her mind around it.

It was stupid, really. Her husband had just died, and she was clearly mad with grief. She must have imagined him talking to her, making up a wild story. Except she knew it was true. She didn't know how or why it worked, but if Brenden was going to come back tomorrow, she needed to move the bones in her yard. She didn't want to be sitting in jail and miss him.

Cecelia moved the bodies out of the hole she dug several years ago, and stashed them underneath her trailer. She winced in pain as she crawled under and started digging. She wouldn't be able to dig far, but she didn't need to. The bodies were mostly bare bones now anyway, and she would have the siding of her trailer repaired right away.

She sat on the steps of her front porch, smoking a cigarette, staring into the darkness. When she went in to grab her cigarettes, Brenden's body was no longer on the couch. He disappeared into nothingness. She missed him terribly. Despite everything, she loved that man. She cried over him for three years, but she didn't cry tonight. She knew he would be back tomorrow. But if that was true, would she remember tonight?

EPILOGUE
AUGUST 2026

A loud knock echoed off the metal walls of Cecelia's bright pink home. When Hurricane Candi hit twenty years prior, the insurance company came through and wrote out a big fat check. Cecelia used the money to have a new home built, out of four shipping containers. It was over twice the size as her old single wide trailer and it was painted pink. The contractor told her the color was actually called "salmon" but she didn't care. She was so happy that she even switched the shade of her lipstick to match it.

Another booming knock echoed throughout her home. She just ordered food through the Door Dash app a half hour ago, and was starving. It was after three, and she still hadn't eaten lunch yet. Even though she had emergency surgery to have her knee replaced several years ago, it still acted up every now and then. It was aching now, so she grabbed her cane. Putting most of her weight on the cane, the seventy-five-year-old woman made her way to the door. She hoped her dasher was a young man. She would tip the ones she found attractive extra, hoping they would become her normal delivery person. She never moved on after Brenden left her, many years ago.

She opened the door, and her jaw locked. The man standing on her front porch wasn't a strapping dasher boy. It was a wrinkled old man; Brenden, her husband. She hadn't seen him in over twenty years, but she recognized him right away. His dark hair was now gray, and he'd lost muscle tone over the years. Cecelia knew he was pushing eighty, but he looked much older. Only his eyes were the same. He had definitely aged, but so had she.

"What the fuck are you doing here?" her voice croaked out, tempted to hit him with her cane.

"I've come home to die," Brenden said, smiling at his wife as he held his arms open to embrace her.

www.ingramcontent.com/pod-product-compliance
Lightning Source LLC
Chambersburg PA
CBHW071155300726
48975CB00004B/1165